AF595689

Demonic encounters

To set the scene this story takes place in a medieval fantasy world. This story features a Black haired cat girl named Mizo and various other characters.

Mizo a black haired neko, cat girl, with ears and tail woke up with a soft yawn. Donning a pair of pink panties with a bow on the front and matching bra, she made sure the underwear was comfortable and stretchy enough to fit her fighting style. Mizo here was classified as a rogue, though she preferred an upfront approach over anything so she was called a "swashbuckler" type. Donning leather armor over her underwear as well as making sure her hair was tied and wouldn't get in the way if combat happened to break out. Taking up her holstered short sword and attaching it to the hip of her armor she stepped out of the inn room and proceeded down the hall. Going down the stairs and into the main room she smiled at the receptionist and exited the inn, her first objective was to get some food from the nearby tavern. And so she walked waving to the townspeople that passed her, Mizo was well known here she was a part of the local guard charged with keeping peace and order. Though some did not look at her with kindness.

Entering the tavern Mizo sat down at one of the tables and ordered a glass of water and some venison with a few fruits, smiling as she did so. While waiting for her food Mizo took the sword from her hip and set it on the table, since she didn't intend to fight anyone in a public area surrounded by civilians. Soon the food was brought to her and it was set down in front of her and the water was set down beside the plate, Mizo gave a happy thank you and adjusted the plate slightly. Mizo was getting ready to eat, when she felt something on the back of her head, and in a moment's notice her head was being pushed down mashing into the plate of food in front of her.

Being surprised like this left her a bit shocked as her face was pressed into the food and moved around a bit, though once regaining her wits she sat up with no resistance and turned her head to find a floating hand behind her head. Mage hand, a spell that makes a spectral hand to move or retrieve things, but this hand was behind the fact her face was now covered in grease. Upon seeing the hand laughter could be heard from another table a voice crying out, **"Looks like someone is a really messy eater!"** another voice called **"Wow Mizo i knew you were a sloppy fighter, but I didn't expect you to be so barbaric with food as well!"** But the next voice that called out is the one that ticked Mizo off. **"Well well, looks like the rogue enjoys stuffing her mouth with meat a bit too much, as expected of a slutty beastkin."**

To this comment Mizo clutched her fist and stood to look at the person responsible for the taunt, a group of elven women was responsible, among them Izunami a high elf that thought she was higher than most others. Izunami's spell book was glowing meaning the spectral hand was her doing, a low growl left Mizo's lips as she reached for her sword only to stop. Letting out a sigh she turned to the women and walked over to them, standing there now with her arms crossed as she looked down to Izunami. **"That's quite enough ruckus from you three."** Mizo said the most stern voice she could manage. **"I can understand if you have a problem with me, but you're disturbing the peace. If you would like to settle a difference then do so on the training grounds. if you wish to meet me there in twenty minutes I would be happy talk with you."** Mizo continued.

Izunami responded in kind **"A chance to actually humiliate you, sure I'd love to show people how beastkin like you should actually be treated!"** the woman then began to laugh. Mizo only responded with a huff as she began to walk back to her table only to feel something slip through her armor. Mizo paused her face flushing pink as the spectral hand tugged on her panties pulling them out of her armor, one of the other elves reacted quickly and dumped their glass of water into the now exposed and pulled panties. This caused Mizo to squeak and quickly pull herself away from the group as they busted out laughing again, Mizo swore under her breath she would teach them a lesson. Mizo grabbed her plate and walked out the door, normally the tavern keeper would have stopped her, but seeing what happened no one bothered.

Taking her meal back to her inn room she quickly changed from the now soaked underwear into a similarly comfortable pair, this time they were pure white and then eating her meal in relative peace. After finishing her meal she picked up the plates and reached for her sword, only for her hand to hit her hip. She had completely forgotten her sword at the tavern. She had to return the dishes anyway, so Mizo picked up the dishes and made her way back to the tavern. Walking up to the tavern keep she handed the dishes back and began to look for her sword only to find it was not where she left it. Knowing she was on a time limit she asked the tavern keeper, **"Pardon me, have you seen a short sword around here? It was at the table I was at earlier."**

And the tavern keeper responded in his deep voice, **"Sorry Mizo, I had seen it, but that elf girl that was messing with you earlier made off with it before I could stop her."**

Mizo gave a heavy sigh as bowed to the tavern keep, paying him for the meal she began to make her way to the training grounds. Upon approaching the training grounds Mizo saw Izunami with her two lackies, the lackeys were standing to the side and one had the sword in hand. Mizo moved to stand opposite of Izunami and glared at Izunami, while Izunami just smirked towards Mizo. Izunami was the first to speak, **"So you decided to finally show up slut! It took you long enough, hope you weren't looking for your sword, my girls decided to look after it for you. You'll get it back, after I humiliate you, like you deserve."** Mizo did not respond; she simply raised her fists in a fighting stance and then rushed at Izunami. Izunami opened her spell book and began to back away, but Mizo was faster taking a swing of her fist, she hardly missed hitting Izunami. Izunami used her chance to cast a firebolt, from point blank Mizo had no choice but to dodge, getting blasted with the heat caused her to back away.

After backing away and quickly checking her wound, to make sure it wasn't serious, she looked to Izunami who had conjured three ice knives and was getting ready to shoot them at Mizo. After a few seconds Mizo rushed again throwing two punches at Izunami, both connecting one to her stomach and the other to her right arm, this caused her to stumble slightly. Izunami then laughed after she choked back the pain and shot the ice knives at Mizo, the first one missed her, but exploded by her leg. Thankfully it wasn't aimed to kill so all it did was cut her armor a bit, the second hit Mizo in her right shoulder causing some damage and then exploded cutting her armor again. Mizo now had a chance and used it to try and punch Izunami again, but Izunami was prepared for her dodging the blow and firing the last knife hitting Mizo in the left side exploding again to cut her armor. Izunami smiled and the lackeys began to laugh in the distance.

Wondering what was going on Mizo looked to them confused and it wasn't until Izunami spoke that Mizo understood, **"Mizo...just wow. To think you couldn't even coordinate that. Who wears a pink bar and white panties..."** Mizo, now thoroughly confused, looked down to see she now stood in her underwear, the ice knives were used to completely cut her armor off, they were aimed at the main straps of the leather she...was wearing. Mizo let out a soft gasp as she ducked down trying to cover herself to no avail. Feeling a familiar feeling from earlier a spectral hand pushed her head and managed to tilt her over so she fell onto the ground. Izunami then placed her heel onto Mizo's head to keep her pressed down on the ground, Mizo only growling in response. **"Hey Mizo, you should stick with your sword, your fist fighting sucks. Anyways, now it's time for the town to know you are a slut."** Izunami said, now motioning for her lackies to do what they had planned. Izunami moved her heel when the group was close, Mizo attempted to get on her feet only to have her own sword pointed to her throat. Mizo froze and glared at Izunami, and Izunami spoke, **"Now you're gonna turn and you're gonna walk into town with us, then your punishment will begin. After today all beastkin like you will be the bottom of the food chain."**

Izunami said this with a loud laugh, now being forced Mizo began to walk towards the town, Mizo knew the roads around here so she closed her eyes and attempted to walk with as much pride as a woman in her underwear could in public. As the group walked into town whispers began to circle them, **"Oh Izunami got to her...poor girl."** said an elderly man, another person in the growing crowd began **"What is going on, why is that woman in**

her underwear. Put on some clothes!" as these whispers gathered around them Mizo's face flushed red. Despite that feeling of embarrassment this wasn't so bad, Mizo thought...if only that had been the end. Izunami shouted, **"Alright girls on three! One! Two! Three!"** Mizo had tried to turn to see what was going, but soon realizing what it was she grit her teeth.

And with the third count Mizo's white panties stretched up her back there were at least five spectral hands holding the back of said panties. Though she grit her teeth she was not prepared for her feet to be raised off the ground, Izunami kept counting and on every three count Mizo was bounced in her underwear in front of the city she protected. Laughter echoed around her, but the only thing she could focus on was the feeling of the panties rubbing against her. Five minutes after being pulled through the air and repeatedly bounced, Izunami spoke **"Well well the city is surely enjoying this, how about you Mizo? I certainly enjoy my view from back here!"** and then began to laugh, her lackeys soon following the laughter as they rapidly bounced Mizo now. Mizo was attempting not to speak, but the taunt caused her to want to say something, Mizo opened her mouth only for a moan to escape her lips. Her face turned deep red as she slightly looked back to the people behind her.

The group of women were staring at her, and Izunami spoke first, **"Hold on. Did...Did you just moan from this?"** Mizo did not respond, yet she didn't fidget or fight, just hanging there in the air while the group was distracted. Izunami snapped and shouted, **"Ok then! Give her what she wants!"** The group responded to this by bouncing Mizo rapidly once again, but doing so yanked her high and let her drop into the cloth of her panties. Mizo could not help herself but moan at the rough handling, only a few minutes passed of this before the panties she was wearing snapped and Mizo landed on the ground holding her crotch. Izunami watched Mizo lay on the ground face first, Mizo's body jolting every now and then. Izunami sighed and gave Mizo's ass a firm slap before speaking, **"Awww guess we ripped them, fun's over**." The group began to walk away , then Izunami walked over to Mizo and whispered, **"Starting tomorrow when you're not on duty you only wear your underwear, you'll pay if you don't...see you tomorrow, slut."**

Izunami laughed happily as she walked away from the now bare bottomed neko, it took Mizo a few minutes before she recovered, standing up she kept her crotch hidden as she walked back to her inn room most people she pasted laughed behind her back due to the walk of shame she had to take. Once back in her inn room she put on a pair of blue panties and changed her bra to match, thankfully she had a spare set of leather armor in her backpack. Getting dressed fully she then looked to the night stand, she never came for briefing so her orders were sent in a letter that was on said night stand. Taking the letter in hand she opened it and began to read it. She had two sections to patrol, around the walls of the city and the other a small route into the forest nearby to check for potential threats. Giving a nod and putting it away she walked out of the room and downstairs yet again, talking to the receptionist, the person handed Mizo a short sword and said Izuanmi had dropped it off.

At least she could hold to her promise of returning it, taking the sword she attached it to the hip of her armor once again, bowed to the receptionist then walked out of the inn. Mizo kept her head down as she walked through town and out of the gate, starting her patrol around the city. All was perfectly fine until she was three fourths of the way through her route. Nearing the end of her route Mizo heard a small noise from around a small corner, taking a peek she found a white haired person with blue horns. **"Hello?"** Mizo asked openly hoping they wouldn't cause trouble, only for their head to turn to Mizo and then a fast jump made it so Mizo looked this person in the eyes. Mizo pulled out her sword in an attempt to threaten the other person, then suddenly the sound of metal clashing, and the breaking was quickly heard. Mizo looked to her sword and only the hilt remained of it, looking back to the person who now held a great axe in hand.

Mizo screamed in fear and fell back onto the ground as the person walked to look her in the eyes. The person was obviously female, but that speed and strength was non-human, the eyes that gazed back at Mizo were blood red. The axe raised slowly and Mizo closed her eyes in response and then a voice spoke, **"Wait hold on. Aren't you the girl that shitty group dragged through the town a little while ago?"** Mizo blinked and blushed deeply to the question yet she responded, **"Wh-What?! No! No way!"** Mizo said loudly attempting to defend herself, and what little honor she had left. The woman then laughed, **"Oh my god you are! You totally are! That shit was priceless! The look on your face when they lifted you off the ground, fucking hell man! ...You know I was gonna kill you...but I think I have a more fun idea."**

Mizo gave a small gulp to the mention of killing her, she breathed slowly and quietly in hopes she wouldn't meet her end here. The woman spoke again, "Here's the deal, take off your armor down to the panties, let me get some anger out then you get to go free." Mizo glared at the women, but hearing this demand Mizo felt two feelings, a threat she had to do this or die, and a willingness to listen from pure...lust maybe? **"Fine..."** Mizo said standing up and moving a bit until her leather armor was now laying on the ground. The woman then took her time and began to walk around Mizo, looking her up and down until she was back at the front again. **"Good good now turn around and get on your hands and knees."** The woman said, and with no hesitation Mizo complied, getting on her hands and knees. Soon she felt the cold knuckles wrap around the back of the waistband of the blue panties and a harsh tug was given. Mizo responded to the tightening of her panties with a loud moan as it rubbed against her crotch, the hand pulled the panties towards her head, though these weren't nearly as stretchy as the others.

The woman began to laugh as she pulled the panties and then spoke, **"Fuck you have a fat ass neko girl! The way it bounces with my pulls is almost beautiful, you were made to get wedgies girl!"** The woman then began to only pull with one hand and with her other she brought it up to bring it down and slap Mizo's pale ass. This one slap left a firm red handprint across her cheeks, this yet again caused Mizo to moan only this time there was no holding back that moan. The woman spoke as she brought her hand down against the pale ass yet again, **"The moan is beautiful! That idiot wasn't joking when she called you a slut! With a moan like that who could resist."** The woman kept spanking Mizo while harshly tugging at the panties, in this process the panties slowly stretched further and further until it stopped around her head. **"Urg...just not enough give to em...! Fuck i wanted the finisher! Fine stand up!"** The woman demanded of Mizo, and Mizo compiled almost too excited to get what the woman was giving her. Now with her red ass Mizo stood there with her back to the woman 'torturing' her. This woman grabbed both sides of the blue panties and pulled up roughly, dragging out another moan from Mizo as the woman snapped the leg holes over Mizo's shoulders then spoke, **"Bam! That was fun! Look at that red ass! Look at the way the panties stretch and bind your arms! One of my best works yet if i can say so. Keep it in, enjoy it. I live in a distant village, so...i'll visit you every now and then, later, loser."**

Mizo stood there wearing her panties over her shoulders, enjoying the feeling while watching the woman walk away. It took her a few minutes to realize the event was over and remove the panties from her shoulder and get her armor back on. Mizo rushed back to the inn to get yet another change of panties after completing her route fully. Once in her room Mizo expected more to come from today and took the time to test how stretchy her next pair was gonna be, if she was gonna be put through it, she definitely wanted to end it right. Selecting a pair of white panties with a bear on the ass she put her armor back on and kept her panties sticking out slightly, in hopes to tempt someone. She had one job left, a quick survey in the woods would take no more than one hour, and so she set on her way. Walking out of the inn she looked to the sky, it was almost night time so she decided to hurry and get this job done with.

Mizo once again walked out of the gates, a new sword in hand, making her way to the forest. This job was meant to be uneventful if nothing happened, but oh was she hoping something happened, with her luck today it would be amazing. Mizo walked around for an hour and sighed, eventually deciding to make her way back to the city, though she eventually passed a log on her way back, deciding to sit for a moment to rest. **"Man, I really wanted something to happen!"** Mizo said with a groan leaning back slightly though soon a voice rang out, **"Does that something had to do with your panties sticking out of your armor?"** A mature woman's voice called out. Mizo blushed heavily as she turned to see who was talking, what Mizo found was a red haired woman dressed in full heavy armor, a red sword by her side, one she recognized very well. **"Co-Commander Lena!"** Mizo shouted as she saluted the woman, Lena just motioned for Mizo to calm down. **"I came out here to check on you, you spent so long on a simple mission I wondered if you were hurt."**

Lena then shifted in her spot with a smirk on her face, **"While i was out shopping for some supplies for the barracks I was told a beastkin with black hair was carried through town by her white undies. After that I looked for you outside the wall and noticed your broken blade. And now here I find you completely fine with your panties showing, Would you like to tell me something soldier?"** While Lena explained this Mizo blushed deeply, time to come clean, **"Well commander...for a full report. Yes I was carried and bounced by my panties until they ripped, then i was going to apprehend someone in an ally outside of town when they broke my sword, they threatened to kill me if I didn't let them use me for anger relief, by this point I just expected to get more wedgies I just left them out...to get it over with quicker...obviously!"** Mizo said this looking at Lena who simply smiled back at Mizo.

Lena spoke once more, **"No no, I get it. You were having fun, but you did keep the peace, in an odd way I'll say. I suppose I should reward you."** Lena paused for a moment before continuing, **"Go ahead take off your armor. If you want wedgies, that's what you'll get."** Mizo gave a gulp as her commander talked, but she did not protest and took off her armor leaving Mizo in her underwear. Lena smiled at Mizo, **"Look at you, you're adorable."** Lena said then sat down on the log and sat beside her. Mizo took the hint and moved next to the commander and for her hand to be grabbed and pulled over the commander's lap. Lena then raised her hand and swatted it against Mizo's ass then spoke. **"That is for making me worry,"** and then another hard slap against the other cheek, **"That's for making fools of the city guard."** and yet another slap, **"And that one is because I love watching your ass bounce."** Lena then pushed Mizo off onto her feet and smirked, **"Tell no one what you see tonight, it'll be our secret, in exchange for keeping your wedgie fetish a secret."** Lena would say looking to Mizo for a response.

Mizo gave a nod in response. She was fidgeting in place, excited to finally get what she wanted, though she didn't actually expect what was coming next. Lena removed her armor until she was in a simple shirt and short, from her back began to form a cloud of darkness, her once gentle green eyes turning fire red. Mizo was speechless as the darkness outstretched into the forms of tentacles with a purple glow to them, Lena then stepped towards Mizo, the tentacles standing by ready to act in a moment. Lena moved behind the neko and pushed her over so Mizo laid over the log, the tentacles moving to keep Mizo laying there. Lena wrapped her hands around the waistband of Mizo's panties, Lena is used to using great weaponry so her strength is humongous, and pulled with all of her might. The panties shot up causing Mizo to moan as it rubbed against her private areas, Mizo's face was deep red. As Lena pulled at the panties the remaining four tentacles that didn't hold Mizo down now hit against Mizo's ass like whips, this caused Mizo to cry out in pain and pleasure. After a few minutes of pulling and spanking Lena let go of the waistband, **"Stretchy, but not good enough yet."** Lena said as the tentacles holding Mizo's wrists let go and wrapped through the leg holes on Mizo's panties.

Quickly the tentacles pulled Mizo into the air making her hang by her panties, this made Mizo moan, obviously. Though Lena didn't stop at lifting her, taking Mizo's ankles in her hands Lena began to pull down on Mizo's legs dragging her deeper into the cloth as the weight and force stretched the panties even more. Lena laughed softly as she pulled Mizo's legs, causing the neko to moan louder the deeper she went into the panties, to add to the neko's pleasure Lena began to let up and cause Mizo to bounce in her hanging wedgie. **"Now that's what I call a wedgie, ready for the big finish Mizo?"** Lena asked looking up to the neko who was rapidly nodding her head. The tentacles lowered Mizo to the ground and Lena dismissed the tentacles and grabbed the back of the waistband again. Lena harshly pulled with all her might again, this time the panties stretched to where she needed them with only a bit of force, and with a shift to move in front of Mizo, Lena pulled the panties over the neko's head letting them snap against Mizo's nose. **"And there you have it. An atomic wedgie for the wedgie slut. You know what, you're on forest night patrol from now on. me and you are gonna have a lot of fun from now on."**

Lena said moving to let Mizo lay on the ground, Mizo held her crotch moaning quietly in her atomic wedgie. Lena put her armor back on and then picked up Mizo's armor and then spoke up again **"I think I'll leave you in the city square overnight like that I'm sure everyone would love to wake up to your ass being humiliated"** Lena hummed happily grabbing onto the thin fabric that was Mizo's panties, placing one hand under Mizo for support Lena now carried Mizo by her wedgie all the way back to town in the dead of night. Lena placed Mizo on the ground and quickly fixed up a *'please spank the wedgie slut - signed, Commander Lena'* then walked away. Mizo laid there on the ground and moaned happily only saying one thing between her monas, **"Best day yet...~!"**

The end.

The Fantasy life of a maid.

This story involves a maid named Zan and her mistress named Alura.

"Mistress!" Shouted a maid as she floated up the staircase to the room where the person she served resided in sleep, **"Mistress! It's time to get up!"** She shouted once knocking on the door before opening it. This maid was a special one, most people would call a floating woman a witch, but this woman was something a bit different, a sorceress by the name of Zan. Zan is a white haired woman with sky blue eyes standing at five foot six inches, she enjoys wearing a nice and simple black and white maid outfit with frills around the white areas. She wears high heels to walk around, mainly because she floats around instead of walking most of the time, her hair goes down past her half back and stops just before her ass. Some part of her hair in the front is braided into a long strand down her right side, a small white flower in her hair just Infront of her maid headdress. The last bit of detail from her outfit would be the ring she wears on her left ring finger that has a small emerald embedded into it, as well as a family crest on her right hand, a mark of ownership, which is a storm cloud with a sword under it. As mentioned before Zan is a sorceress with control over wind and weather type elements, using this power allows her to fly if she wished or make other things float, a neat trick to have sometimes.

Zan knocked on the door three more times then sighed softly as she opened the door slowly, **"I'm coming inside milady."** Zan would say loudly as she looked into the room blushing slightly. Her eyes scanned the room checking to see if the mistress was playing tricks on her, but the moment she saw the bed Zan let out a sigh. Yep there she was in the bed, asleep, as usual. Zan walked over to the bed and looked down to the woman sleeping inside of it, **"It's time to get up Mistress Allura."** She said reaching to gently shake the sleeping woman. The woman sat up with a loud yawn closely following her sitting up, **"I'm up, I'm up..."** The woman muttered quietly. Allura Stormflank, the mistress of the house Zan worked under and Zan's best friend ever since she was employed for the Stormflank family. Allura is a woman with blonde hair and green eyes who is just a bit taller than Zan by about two inches. The woman was twenty three years old, only two years older than Zan. Allura has long wavy hair, very soft to the touch and well taken care of, her closet is full of all kinds of clothing she also has all kinds of jewelry, but hardly ever wears it. Unlike Zan, Allura has no special skills, talents, or magic. Allura was simply a noble who inherited riches and used them to help people around her. Normally Allura kept up a good view to the public for her noble name, but at home she was less so, Allura is rowdy and playful in the privacy of her home.

Zan looked over her mistress and shook her head a bit, **"Milady, why do you insist on only sleeping in your underwear?"** Zan asked, blushing softly. Allura responded with a quiet, **"Cause it's comfy."** Allura then let out yet another yawn. Zan sighed again and moved to Allura's closet and began to pick out an outfit for the noble talking as she did, **"Well you need to hurry and get up, breakfast is almost ready the other maids have been working tirelessly to meet my standards. After breakfast you have some free time, I suggest some shopping for some more comfortable night clothing, after that you have a meeting with the twin rulers from the castle, after the meeting we need to go**

over the checklist for maid duties some of them are slacking with chores, after that you should be free for the rest of the day." Zan said all of this while picking out clothing for the woman, placing them on the bed in front of her. **"Yeah..."** Allura said a few times throughout Zan's talking, in truth she wasn't listening at all to the maids rambling, she didn't even notice the clothes in front of her. Zan then walked out and closed the door behind her, **"I'll be out here until you get changed, milady."**

Zan stood with her back to the door and waited patiently, Zan reflected on how things were right now. The capital, called Borealis, was peaceful after the king passed on, there were no plans on war, no in fighting and now a pair of twins, one male and one female, jointly ruled over the kingdom. Zan herself wasn't born in the kingdom, instead she fled from her home in the west and was found in the city by Allura's father who took her in as a worker in exchange for free housing and food. Back then the west was enveloped in war with the south and Zan lost her family in a surprise attack from the enemy, she was the only one to escape, but she can hardly remember that day, besides the fire from the buildings. Zan shook her head and then sighed, she turned back to the door and knocked on it, **"Are you done getting dressed Allura?"** Zan asked, being a bit more casual with her mistress' name. Though no response came from the room, Zan once again opened the door and quickly spotted Allura laying back in the bed on her side cuddling one of her larger pillows.

Zan angrily walked over being quiet as she did, she wanted to shout at her friend, but felt since maids were nearby she shouldn't do that. Zan walked back to the door and quietly closed it, she then walked back to her sleeping mistress and moved the covers off of her. This exposed Allura in her bright pink panties and matching bra to the maid, Zan quietly said, **"I'll teach you to wake up on time..."** Zan said putting her left knee on the bed, she reached her hands towards her mistress' panties and subtly slipped her hands under the waistband of the bright pink cloth. This is where Zan showed she was more of a friend than a maid to Allura, this wasn't Zan's preferred way of waking up her mistress, but it certainly was effective. Zan pressed her weight on the knee on the bed and quickly yanked the pink cloth into the air pulling Allura along with them, Allura quickly gasped as she was awakened and pulled by her panties. The pink cloth tightened on Allura's crotch and the back slipped between her cheeks, Zan then used one hand to keep the panties there and gave Allura's exposed rear a firm slap. While Zan was doing this Allura was shifting tiredly groaning at the odd wake up, soon feeling the hand hit her rear she gave another small gasp and called out, **"I'm up! I'm up! I'm serious this time! Let me go!"**

Zan smirked and let go of her mistress' panties, letting the woman nearly faceplant on the bed, **"Good, change your panties, get dressed and meet me downstairs for breakfast."** Zan would say with a pleased smile and walk out of the room and down the stairs. Allura groaned, picking her wedgie and rubbing her ass a bit from the slap, **"Jerk."** She said quietly before following the instructions her maid gave her, Allura got dressed in a nice cotton sweater under a simple blue dress which was affixed under her chest. Allura left her room with an air of regalness and pride as if her rude wake up call had never actually happened. Allura made her way downstairs and to the kitchen where Zan waited with a smile on her face holding a tray filled with food from omelets to arranged fruits. Once Allura sat down Zan set the plate in front of the mistress, **"Here you are mistress Allura. Today's breakfast is brought to Nina, one of our new maids. Try not to go too hard on her, she tried really hard."** Allura picked up her utensils and began to taste the food Infront of her, after a few bites of each food she set the utensils down and sighed. Allura waited a moment before she spoke, **"The fruits are fruits, it's hard to mess up...but the omelet,**

get this out of my sight, it's disgusting." Allura said, pushing the plate away from her.

To this response Zan let out a soft sigh, taking the omelet and moving it away and bringing back a different one to set it in front of Allura. **"I expected this would happen even if I gave her my recipe, so I made one of my special ones just for you today mistress."** Zan smiled as Allura picked up her utensil and began to eat with no further problems. Zan moved to the actual kitchen and gave the maid, Nina, the bad news that she messed up the food. Zan gave her a pat on the back and simply suggested she try something easier next time. Zan set up the workers table to let the other servants eat, and then moved back to Allura, Zan sat down at the table beside Allura with a smile on her face. **"I'm happy you enjoy the food I prepared for you Allura, I love cooking for you."** Allura glared to Zan, **"Zan, meet me in my room after breakfast."** Zan gave a nod not changing her tune whatsoever, **"As you wish milady."** Zan said then quietly ate some of the fruits Allura had not touched yet. Zan was a picky eater sometimes and her preferred foods were fruits, she tended to keep to sweeter fruits, but stayed away from strawberries due to allergies.

After eating breakfast Allura stood up and looked at Zan, Zan stood up and called to Nina, **"Nina! Please come clean up the mistress' plates, I have something I need to attend to."** Nina, a brunette maid with glasses, rushed out of the other room and saluted Zan. **"No need for that dear, just say alright."** Nina gave a nod, just then Allura grabbed Zan's wrist and began to drag Zan back to Allura's room, Zan using her magic to float so she was easier for her mistress to pull along. Entering Allura's room Zan closed to the door and locked it behind them, as she expected to be told to do, Zan motioned to it when Allura looked back to her. Allura growled softly under her breath and stood proudly in the middle of the room, she then pointed to Zan, who was just smiling like a dumbass, and spoke, **"Dress off. Now."** Zan still smiled though blushing deeply as she began to remove her dress, this left her in her pure white panties and bra. Allura then moved to the side of her bed and sat down, she patted her lap expecting Zan to know what to do, and Zan simply did as she was expected to, Zan moved to Allura and laid down across her legs. It wasn't unnatural for Allura to want alone time with Zan, the two were very close friends, ones who didn't mind playing around with each other. Now having Zan lay across her lap Allura moved her hand to gently rub Zen's left ass cheek, before quickly giving the cheek a firm slap, this slap caused Zan to groan softly. **"That's for waking me up with a wedgie."** Allura would say, before moving her hand to Zan's other cheek, and giving that an even harder slap. Allura spoke once more **"And that's for making me taste test that omelet, did you even check it?"** Allura said accusing Zan of being lazy, which Zan retorted, **"Of course I checked it milady, but to suffer alone would be boring."** Zan said with a smile still on her face.

"That's even worse of an answer than simply not checking it you dolt!" Allura shouted before slapping both of Zan's cheeks once again as hard as she could manage which caused Zan to groan once then moan to the second slap. Zan giggled at the reaction of her mistress, though soon found herself on a more involving 'punishment.' Allura growled quietly and grabbed the back of Zan's white panties and pulled up on them causing the fabric to tighten around Zan's crotch. The wedgie caused Zan to moan quietly and lower her head, Allura pulled in spades never one after the other to make the maid moan softly each time she pulled rather than a constant moaning. Allura was blushing deeply now as she spoke, **"Yeah...You like that don't you, naughty maid!"** Allura would say with a slight aggression to her voice, she was asserting her dominance yet again. Allura pulled harder and harder with each time, each pull causing the fabric to tighten and pull against Zan's crotch. **"Urg~! Yes I like it a lot mistress!"** Zan called out as she blushed deeply shifting slightly, Allura smirked as she pushed Zan gently to shift her so she was sitting on her knees on the floor. Allura then placed both of her feet on Zan's shoulders and used them to push Zan back as she pulled the panties harder, the force of this caused Zan to moan louder than before, thankfully the room was soundproof. The cloth tightened even more, showing off Zan even more as the cloth popped and stretched, soon enough Allura began to pull it a bit more down causing Zan to lower her head a bit more.

"Pull your head up now!" Allura said with a demanding voice, Zan followed her order and raised her head and with a few more tug of the fabric with harsh force Allura managed to get the waistband to snap against Zan's head. Zan gave a small groan feeling the tight panties snap on her forehead, she now looked up to her mistress in an embarrassed state. Allura smiled down looking at her work, looking upon Zan, the head maid, sitting there in an atomic wedgie basically begging for more. Allura smiled and stood up from her spot and walked around to Zan's back, Allura then unclipped Zan's bra and let it fall to the floor and then spoke, **"Look at you Zan, that must be so embarrassing for you~ Honestly I think it fits your naughty behavior to be punished like this. But I think you want more...don't you?"** Allura asked this, reaching back and slapping Zan's ass yet again, which drew a strained moan from Zan's lips. **"Ye-yes, I do mistress..."** Zan spoke hesitantly and Allura responded with a giggle she moved to her drawer and grabbed something from it, Zan knew it all too well, the collar they used in private. Allura then came to Zan and locked the collar around her neck, a lead in her hand connected to said leash, **"Come on then."** Allura then began to slowly walk around the room, forcing Zan to follow her by crawling moaning with how the movement made the atomic wedgie shift. After five minutes of this Allura removed the collar and tossed it to the side, Allura then bent down to Zan and whispered, **"My my, despite how you look, you still have your beauty."** Allura then pulled the panties off of Zan's head to let them snap back against her lower back. **"I enjoyed playing with you Zan, I love you."** Zan blushed stuttering from both pleasure and embarrassment, **"I-I L-love you t-to mistress."** Allure cupped her hand under Zan's chin and gently kissed her, in all fairness, Allura was definitely the dominant one between the two.

Though this didn't happen most days, this was only the morning, and there was a lot more to come from the day.

The end.

Secret under the moonlight.

This small story once again involves Mizo and a red haired human female named Lena.

As the sun set over the city Lena, the red haired warrior commander and leader of the guards, stood by the gate waiting. The great sword Lena had was sheathed and strapped to her back, the handle sticking out over her right shoulder. Lena would normally be wearing her heavy armor, but today was a rather special day so instead she wore a simple white T-shirt and cloth pants. Lena tapped her foot on the ground as she waited, her arms crossed, she was waiting on Mizo again. This had been a constant occurrence now ever since the first day Mizo became the town's wedgie slut, which was fine and all, it just made Mizo late to her job a lot. Lena felt a tinge of cold on her shoulder, feeling as if Mizo was not going to show. Lena's eyes drifted into the city streets, a soft sigh escaping her lips, expecting to have to go alone she turned her back to the city square. Though the moment Lena turned her back and was about to start walking a voice called out.

"Commander! Don't leave without me please!" Cried a voice behind Lena from a distance, Lena turned her head to check who it was, but Lena knew exactly who it was. Turning to look at the voice's directly Lena spotted the very familiar black haired beastkin, or neko if you prefer. Mizo, the town guard recently turned into a public wedgie slut thanks to Lena honestly though she did indeed keep her job on the guard thanks to Lena. Mizo ran up with her short sword strapped to her hip like usual, though thanks to previous events Mizo hardly wore her armor anymore, choosing to walk about simply in her underwear since they'd be revealed anyways. "I'm sorry for being late again Commander Lena! I had another run in with Izunami...she stretched my last pair of panties really thin so I wanted to get a new pair you could have fun with later!" Mizo said this proudly proclaiming what had happened, almost too happy to admit her own humiliation.

"Yes yes," Lena retorted, "I know you had your fun, but don't you think you should take your job a bit more seriously? What if I had gotten hurt?" Lena ended moving one hand to her hip the other hanging to the side as she glared at the neko. Mizo gave an angry look to this response and replied, "Well I would track them down and make them pay! A-After making sure your ok of course." Mizo said this, afraid she would get yelled at for not thinking of making sure Lena was ok first. Lena simply shook her head and walked to where she was beside Mizo, giving the beastkin's ass a firm slap, Lena began to walk out of the gate. Mizo let out a small yelp to being spanked by the commander, and watching Lena walk a few steps Mizo began to follow her commander. Lena walked along their usual forest route, the total trip on their route would take a few hours at best until the sun went down and the moon was decently high in the sky.

While they were walking Mizo spoke up with a question for her commander, "So Commander Lena, where is your armor?" Mizo had asked, eyeing up her commander's form from behind. Lena didn't look back though she did respond, "My armor had gotten a bad dent in it due to the new trainees practice. They knocked a weapon rack over, I made sure no one got harmed by throwing myself in the way, thankfully no one, including me, was injured." Lena said this, though it wasn't true at all, the new trainees were under a different guard's watch today so she had nothing to do with the incident. Though Mizo gasped softly, "Wow! That's amazing of you captain! We are so grateful to have you around!" Mizo said with the most honest and impressed tone Lena had heard so far from the neko. Lena let out a quiet sigh, of course Mizo hadn't known due to being busy getting her panties pulled all day long, but the redhead decided to retort, "Now you know where my armor is, so where's the rest of your clothing? Last I checked you needed to be in your uniform to go on missions."

Hearing the commander mention this Mizo's face turned a bit red, "Well I mean...my underwear is just gonna end up on display anyways, so what's the use for clothes...?" While Mizo said this she looked away from the commander, though Lena wasn't going to let this slip by so easily, "So you decided since you the public wedgie slut, it was a good idea to just go out in your underwear and meet up for an important route to look for problems?" Mizo gave a small yelp in response to the reply the commander gave her, "Uh, well, i-i...um..." Mizo began to mumble thinking she had gotten into trouble and was about to be actually punished. Lena simply began to laugh in response, "Calm down Mizo, I was just playing around, I know why your went out in your underwear, and I know I can protect you, so I don't mind." Lena said this with a smile on her face while reaching back and patting the great sword on her back. Hearing this Mizo gave a very audible sigh of relief.

The two walked for hours eventually coming to a familiar log on the ground, this was where Lena had found Mizo and where Lena had given the neko the actual title of wedgie slut. Lena sat down on the log, she let her bag fall from her side behind the log, Mizo stood in front of Lena smiling and blushing, she was obviously expecting something. Lena stretched her arms while closing her eyes only to open one to look at Mizo, "What?" Lena asked, "Oh right...well before that I brought something for you. It's in my bag one second." Lena said shifting and bending over the log to start going through her bag. The moment Lena did this Mizo blushed even more watching the commander's ass wiggle in the cloth clothing that was her pants. Mizo waited patiently, while watching the decently sized ass wiggle in front of her. Come to think of it, Mizo had never seen the commander without her armor until tonight. Feeling an urge rise in her chest Mizo raised her hand up and froze, she was fighting with her mind over what she should do. 'I should just wait' she thought to herself, 'but then I will NEVER get this chance again' she responded to her own thought, 'if I do it I'm sure to get punished' a moment of silence in her mind. 'It's worth being punished!' she thought, closing her eyes as she brought down her hand against Lena's ass.

Lena's body jolted, feeling the hand hit against her rear, her face turning a bit red, Lena took her attention away from the bag and looked back to Mizo. Mizo's ears were flat on her head now, staring at Lena with almost fear in her eyes, Lena however looked away from Mizo and mumbled, "Ag..." Mizo blinked at her commander's reaction and relaxed herself looking at how Lena was laying on the log now, "Wh-What?" Mizo responded with hesitation. Lena groaned quietly, "Again...do it...again." Lena said, looking away from Mizo not wanting to show her embarrassed face to the lower ranking soldier. "Uh sure?" Mizo responded with a confused tone, Mizo raised her hand and brought it down against Lena's ass once more, but on the opposite cheek. This slap was met with Lena giving a quiet squeak, her body jolting once again from the slap, Lena now placed her hands on the ground and wiggled her hips. Mizo smiled watching her commander shift in her space, but was more surprised when Lena wiggled her hips, Mizo knew what she wanted. So Mizo gave the commander what she was asking for.

Mizo moved to the side of her commander, bringing her hands up and then spanking Lena time and time again, five total on each cheek before something changed. Mizo spanked the fifth time to meet by the quiet squeak of her commander, to add a bit of salt to the wound Mizo was openly counting how many times she spanked each cheek. "Time for number six Lena!" Mizo said happily not even using her commander's title anymore, Mizo brought her hand up and once again brought it down against Lena's ass. A decently loud clap sounded around them with the spank, but the next noise was more of a surprise, "Ah~!" A moan had left the commander's lips, Lena was now looking directly at the ground to not look at Mizo as she was spanked. "Well, well." Mizo said looking down to her commander, "Was that a moan? If I didn't know any better I would think you enjoy this~ But I think I can make it better!" Mizo said shifting a bit, Mizo moved her hands to her commander's waistband of her pants. "Don't you dare Mizo!" Lena cried out, though she didn't even attempt to move or stop the neko from doing what she planned. "Don't dare do what? It's not my fault your loose pants fell down while you were wiggling about!" Mizo would say pulling the pants of her commander down to the woman's ankles. Lena was happy her face was pretty much hidden, because she was embarrassed to hell and back.

Mizo giggled as the pants of her commander slid down with no trouble at all, she gazed at her commander's smooth legs and eyed her all the way up until she moved her eyes onto the panties her commander was wearing. Mizo's face went a deep red, Lena had chosen a rather odd choice of underwear, Lena was wearing a pair of purple panties with frills all around them that showed off her ass. Mizo moved back a bit, "Wow, those look really pretty...on your...red ass." Lena would groan and speak "Oh shut up..." Which Mizo would retort "Oh? You're going for something pretty knowing I would start spanking you tonight? No wonder you were wiggling all around luck that, pervert!" Mizo said this giggling a bit at the end, Lena groaned pushing herself off the log to stand up, she looked at Mizo with her pants still around her ankles. "I have mature panties, congrats, a grown woman wears grown ass panties, what a surprise." Lena said, shaking her hands in the air before bending over and pulling her pants back up. "Awww I thought we were having fun!" Mizo said disappointed that her spanking session was over. Lena picked up her bag and looked at Mizo, she spoke calmly, yet hesitation was in her voice. "I...have one more stop before we go back to the city. Come on."

Lena began to walk without warning and Mizo was soon following after her, Mizo however decided to try and tease Lena as they walked, "So, Lena, Are we gonna be alternating now? One night you wedgie me, another I spank you till you...you know~" To this Lena did not respond and eventually Mizo fell silent not knowing what Lena had planned for her tonight. Lena led Mizo through the forest until eventually the two reached a gap in the trees, stepping through the two found themselves in front of a large lake, the moon reflecting on the surface of the water. Mizo looked over the scene in awe, while Lena looked to Mizo for her reaction, and other reasons, Mizo began, "Whoa, that is so pretty, when did you find this commander?" Lena responded with "Just Lena, right now I am not your commander, I'm simply your friend." Lena then gently grabbed Mizo's hand and pulled her to an open area where they could sit down and rest after all the walking. "I found it a few nights ago while I was on a walk after our route, it made me think of you, and how much I wanted to bring you here." Lena said pulling her bag into her lap, Lena then pulled out a small box and resumed, "Mizo I bought you something a few days back and I've wanted to give it to you for awhile now, and now I think I'm ready to." Lena then handed the small box to Mizo, which Mizo happily took and opened. Inside was a necklace that had the word 'Wedgieslut' in small blocks.

Mizo smiled and happily put it on with no hesitation, "I love it...Lena." Mizo said looking over to Lena, and Lena responded, "Well, I love you Mizo." And in that moment Mizo froze. "Wait? What?" Mizo said with a confused look on her face, Lena looked back to her. Lena's face was deep red with a happy smile on it, "I love you Mizo." Lena repeated, then continued, "I've loved you for a while now, but I could never get the words out while I was stretching your panties." Lena sighed and looked towards the ground, "Yeah I get it, I'm the commander of the guard, I'm seen as a brute, unlovable, and to boot I'm a demon. But I thought maybe I could-" Mizo then interrupted, "Shut up idiot." Lena looked towards Mizo about to ask a question only for the neko to press her lips to Lena's lips. Lena was shocked for a moment, eventually closing her eyes, Mizo shifted and placed herself in Lena's lap, both girls blushing as they kissed. The kiss went on for a few seconds...minutes...hours? Neither of them was sure how long it went on for, but one thing was for sure, Lena broke this kiss in her own way. Getting to the point of struggling to breath from the kiss Lena grabbed onto Mizo's waistband of her panties and pulled them up from the back, these actions caused Mizo to lean and moan. "What the hell are you thinking dumbass! Don't surprise me like that!" Lena shouted as she repeatedly tugged on the yellow panties.

Mizo moaned in response to the wedgie she was getting but managed to respond, "I'm sorry, but you kept talking negatively about yourself and I couldn't take it anymore! You are a wonderful person Lena, demon, brute, or otherwise! I love you the way you are!" Mizo shouted in response. Lena stopped pulling the panties at the response, "So...will you be mine?" Lena asked not thinking before she spoke, Mizo smiled happily and nodded in response to the question. Lena smiled brighter than ever before, she moved one hand to the neko's ass gripping it gently, the other hand tugging the panties upward. Mizo wrapped her legs around Lena's waist, refusing to be pulled off the woman's lap. Lena pulled and tugged the panties until they stretched enough and snapped the waistband over Mizo's forehead, Lena then kissed Mizo holding her tightly. Mizo held onto Lena moaning the entire time, her moaning stopping when the atomic wedgie was fulfilled. Breaking the kiss Lena spoke, "Hey...hun. Get off, don't pick the wedgie I want you to keep it in. I have a surprise so close your eyes for a bit." Mizo gave a nod to Lena and closed her eyes. There was a bit of shuffling noises, the sound of unclipping, and then reclipping after a few seconds. "Ok I'm ready." Lena said Mizo then opened her eyes to find Lena standing there in only a bar and a pair of white panties.

Lena's body has several scars from battle, one going up her left leg, her right arm had an almost circular cut on it, and her back had a very large burn scar. Mizo didn't mind any of these scars, it made it even more impressive honestly. Lena then motioned to the new panties she had on, "Have fun I guess?" She said Mizo took the hint rather quickly, undoing her atomic she went behind Lena grabbing the back of the waistband. Mizo giggled and pulled up on the plain white panties, which made Lena grunt as the panties tightened, "Urg...how can you enjoy that?" Lena asked shifting the panties a bit, but Mizo didn't respond, the neko simply continued to pull and dig the panties further into Lena's crotch. "Ok ok I get it, I'm wedged, haha. You can let go now." Lena said hesitantly, Mizo responded, "Oh no, these babies are going atomic babe!" Lena replied with a silent 'fuck' as Mizo began to pull harder and hard. Mizo eventually grabbed Lena's hand, leading her over to a nearby branch. Lena moved both her and Mizo up to the branch Mizo then hooked Lena's panties on the branch and pushed the red head off. Lena let out a soft yelp in fear as she fell but was caught by her panties digging into her once again, stopping her fall.

"Urg! Fuck!" Lena shouted as she held her crotch, Mizo then spoke, "Oh babe, your gonna be sore tomorrow from that~! But we aren't done, they aren't stretched enough!" Mizo said grabbing Lena's ankles and starting to pull down on them. Mizo started bouncing Lena in the hanging wedgie to help stretch the fabric of the panties. After a few minutes of this Mizo went back up and unhooked Lena from the branch letting the read head fall to the ground not far below her at this point. Mizo didn't give Lena a chance and quickly grabbed the waistband again and pulled it as hard as she could making Lena squeak as the cloth moved over the back of Lena's head and Mizo gently set it against the woman's forehead.

"Atomic wedgie!" Mizo shouted happily, Lena sighed standing slowly while holding her crotch. "So you want me to walk back in this huh?" Lena asked only for Mizo to give rapid nods, Lena then continued, "Fine, but I have to so do you." Mizo smiled then quickly pulled her own panties back over her head, the two then carefully gathered their stuff and began the long track back to town. Approaching the gate Lena spoke up, "From now on don't bother with that inn, your staying with me, my little nerd." Mizo then responded, "Of course honey, i wouldn't have it any other way." Walking through the town streets in the dead of night so Lena was spared the humiliation thankfully. As the two got ready for their rest, Mizo got settled in and the two decided to sleep only in their underwear Lena spoke up once more, "You know, after awhile that wedgie doesn't feel too bad." Mizo retorted, "Soooooo i can wedgie you more often?" To which Lena sighed kissing the neko, "Only in private my dear." Lena said getting a giggle out of Mizo, the two cuddled and soon fell into slumber.

The end.

A note from Mizo:

Hey there! Thank you for reading the stories I published. I really appreciate it! I know these small collections are not much in the way of a book, but this is what I have been working on for a long time now!

While I was making this book and trying to get things worked out, my life is not going in the best direction and when that happens to me I try to make people smile even more!

So I hope you found joy in this odd little book of mine! I look forward to writing more content and doing much more to make people happy!

www.ingramcontent.com/pod-product-compliance
Lightning Source LLC
LaVergne TN
LVHW041259150826
845673LV00008B/2653